(UN)ERASED: EMOTIONS LAST

KAIF ABBAS

Made with ♥ on the Notion Press Platform
www.notionpress.com

To me,

From me.

Contents

INTRODUCTION

There are times in life when you wish to run away—from the world, from your environment, from your life, and even from yourself. Life is full of uncertainty and unimaginable situations.

This book is as raw as it can be. There is no attention to grammar, no usage of "appropriate" words, and no focus on punctuation. It is just the flow of thoughts. You know what? When I sat down to try to compile all my thoughts in the form of a book, I had this opportunity to edit, rewrite, and change everything; I even thought of doing so, but then I dropped this idea.

Like a stream of water that is left to create its own path, I left behind my sense of good grammar and even the use of punctuation. I left them, and I left my thoughts free.

Over the few pages that you read, you might find some references to "LIGHT". This is a reference to someone I would not like to disclose, at least at this moment. Maybe, in future editions of this book, I will replace the word "LIGHT" with a name that might actually make more sense. For now, you are free to substitute any name of your choice in place of "LIGHT".

I have been through certain phases and know how our mind can haunt us and how hard it can be to deal with the world and ourself at the same time. Things are getting better now. Writing has helped me get over a lot of things, express the unexpressable, and deal with the undefinable.

I hope after reading the pages of the book, you will find them relatable if you have been through similar experiences of losing everyone you ever loved and every friend you ever trusted. I wonder how people just leave or change? Months ago, they were not able to live without you, and all of a sudden, they do not need you anymore. I wonder if they are able to sleep peacefully at night!

I have cared for everyone except myself. And this is the reward that I got—a reward in the form of beasts haunting my mind—nightmares, flash tears, and flashbacks. At times we feel banished, abandoned, or left, and those are the times when we want someone to be by our side, to listen if we have something to share, or just stay there without leaving. There is a strong desire to be hugged, held, and to have someone approach you to wipe your tears and griefs away. Unfortunately, all of your fantasies and desires serve no purpose other than to aggravate your distress.

There are millions and millions of people on earth, and suddenly, when you look out for someone who is looking for you, I wonder why the world goes empty. Why has this book's content not been revised and proofread? because I do not want to alter the rawness of the words written. I want you to read exactly how I went out looking for solace and peace and how I returned with grief and without ease. Those were dark, fearful times. I see that when you are left in one place and you know this is where you need to stay, maybe forever, you learn to survive; perhaps so have I.

When it comes to emotions, they are the last to make decisions for your life. They have control over you, and they are the ones who guide your way. They are the ones who will determine whether you are left crying or smiling. However strong your resolutions have been, however strongly you have made up your mind to not give up, emotions have the final say. Perhaps this is why people give up on their lives, isn't it? I consider them not to be weak enough; they fought, and they fought beyond the threshold of their bearable strength. They eventually gave up because their emotions took over. How difficult and strange it is, and how strange it is that it is so well known!

Emotions are also the ones that last forever. The thoughts that have penetrated deep into your heart and caused it to hurt both emotionally and physically—those are the unforgettable emotions; they are eternal. Perhaps this is why, while we can theoretically erase emotions by finding a new hobby or setting a goal, they are not truly erasable—at least for me. And now you know why the book is titled "(Un)Erased: Emotions Last."

I hope you find this book to be successful in conveying sense, senselessly!

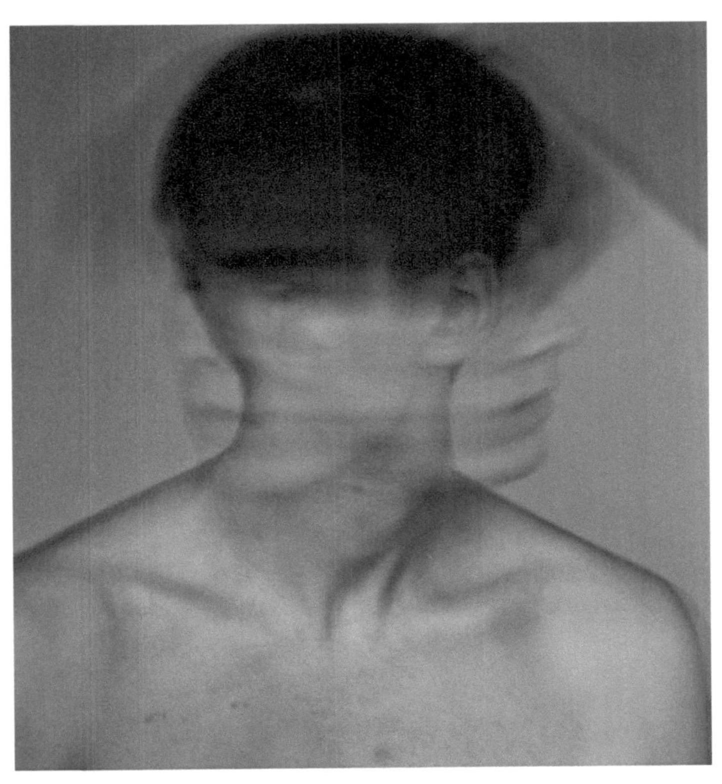

I

Crazed

For me inspiration is time dependent...
"In the end you have to face and stand alone...."
that's all I know...

ℵ

...be waiting for you to wish me... and maybe feel myself wrapped around you....
...In the arms of someone. Sitting around fire, on a cold winter night with tiny stars trying to peep through the pouring fog.

ℵ

...I posted something, wrote then erased, wrote again and erased again... and finally removed the post...

ℵ

...There are certain people you wish to run back into... you want them to be there... and then when you call for them, in the exact moment you realize how drastically they changed...

ᘓ

That is this when one withdraws the howl...

So did I....

It is not about initiating and bending down a little... realize this, people don't get affected by what you do... but the way you say certain things... the way you frame your sentence/ phrase...

Things change!

My love story with you is such that even the stories of fairies would envy...

ᘓ

The feeling of your presence is revolving around me so much, that nothing affects...

We will be meeting really soon... The journey [left] is very less. And whenever you hugged me... you held me close and tight... and I used to ask you to loosen your hold on me...

That day where eternity is no more an illusion, when you hug me like you did/do... I won't ask you to lose your hold...

Had enough for your physical absence...

That day angels would know, and skies too... and thunder and rains...

What is called, falling in love with all heart, soul, mind and body...

And I am always first yours and then anyone else'...

It is said, "I love you to the moon and back". If you look at distance then I should say I love you to the Neptune and back or maybe to the extremist arm of the Milky Way and back...

What best is that when I hug you, you don't withdraw yourself unless I lose my arms...

And for me, I can hold you close, the moment on till eternity...

But then, had you been there...

[This quote]" If I am gone, you won't come looking for me..". that was so true...

I said it someday that If I ever go missing from faceboook, you'll never bother finding me out.

There are just two things there and that is, either I have me or I don't...

swaying between two of them...

I frequently get to hear that I do not speak normal and phrases like "something is unusual about you." "something strange in your ways of speech and presence."

I tell them, I am not present. Why? All in me is all you. I call you my soul. Alive is delusional.

II

Lunatic

I always thought people give way to reason, remain on a point, but they don't.

I assumed, that everyone is a human, feels and has love. Nobody. Nobody has.

I guess there are certain people who could stab without a thought.

When I compare them with people I personally know, there is such a huge difference. So much.

Completely shocked!

My being here has given so much different aspects of people. I would have hardly ever found.

I guess devil has taken human forms and defames humanity.

ᘓᘐ

When someone receives a thing without craving for it, begging (kind of) and trying, their sub-conscious mind feel that it is not good for them or not made for them....

Therefore their in-built protection makes them to turn their backs....

This is where they blunder in life and later regret....

One of my favorite poetess Emily Dickinson in one of her poems says, "The heart wants what it wants-or else it does not care."

I haven't heard many stories, but yeah, I am aware of all the popular fairy tales- Rapunzel, Snow White, Cinderella, Sleeping Beauty, Alice...

One thing that resonates well with fairy tales and real life is that; in reality there is no shoe, no prince, no princess, no magical hairs, no white rabbit, but one thing will always be there and that is- "a poisoned apple."

No matter what, like Emily said, "The heart wants what it wants-or else it does not care."

Just, it gets too late, at times,

and sometimes so much that it gets impossible to return back. I heard Jaun Elia who is one such poet who goes really emotional towards the end of his poem.

Time doesn't stops....

I would dedicate this to someone special... and the "this" is that in the end nothing remains with me except you LIGHT...

My atoms are all yours... you live in my eyes and you flow in my blood...

I haven't said anything as explicit as this...

LIGHT... beyond limits, I remember [miss] you... I love you beyond limits... beyond anything...

I'll meet you soon... I know... You must be waiting to meet me, even more...

I want to talk with you about a lot of things.... a lot of them...

I think of you all the time... all the time...

if it is someone I consider close to myself, it is because I think that very person would be [like] you... but there is none... [Only] you are you...

These [poems] are all written in your memory...LIGHT had you been near to me [physically], I would have narrated them to you in my [voice]... and you would have been left to smile through the day... and I would just see you...

Lest, you know my behaviour and I know you...

Yours December...

P.S. this is because someone made me realize that there is no more feel in the world...

People leave without a thought...

Heavens! This is an everyday thing now.

I write and then erase.... again write and again erase...

I run in madness, looking everything, everywhere...

Had you been there...

No matter who-so-ever says anything.... I have always learnt this... everyone is alike....

Everyone is just the same... everyone is everyone.....

Everyone, everyone, everyone, everyone...

I say world isn't a good place and every time I say this, I find it is being proved right...

And never say to me "I am there"... I repeat NEVER...

All I want is to scatter myself in you...

And how much I wish you to be here...
Had you been there!

Like you did then, do when at times I wish I were able to hug you and burry myself in you...

but had you been there!... it won't have changed my heart beat to tell them that...

I know... you would have not allowed anyone to even look at me sternly....

But all of this is kept in debt... when I turn up in Heavens someday.... Be there to take me...

Then.... let not then any angels get near me, let not them to speak to me...

Tell them, I am all yours..

I am there, again with you...

God knows how much your being miss from me... [Sad]

Had you been there!

I remember you in a way, that even without any intention or without a thought [about you], my tears start to flow...

When I needed you... I never found you...

ꟷ

Had you been there to see what happens... [Sad]

ꟷ

III

Disturbed

And at times I really miss you... I just want to put my fingers on your cheeks and feel your face... *[Sad]*...

Everyone leaves but not you...

Had this been possible but if only God permits... *[Sad]*

And sometimes I wish you could understand...

And sometimes you could see none but me...

And sometimes your world could have shrunk in me...

And sometimes the love in mine eyes could have made you drunk...

And sometimes you did notice how I stare at you...

And sometimes you could ask how I am going...

Sometimes you could have hugged me without a reason...

Or maybe sometimes (out of nowhere without context) you could have said that you love me..

And sometimes you could run your fingers in mine hairs...

And sometimes you could make me properly dress...

Sometimes (maybe) you could fight with me just to tease...

And sometimes you could have assured you are just mine...

And you could allow me to escape in you...

Sometimes I'd sleep in your arms...

Sometimes I did cook for you and you appreciate...

And sometimes you could bear the kid in me...

Sometimes I would act stubborn and you did explain...

And sometimes you could offer me remote for a Doreamon Premier and I did make you maggi so we could see and watch together...

And sometimes I'd explain what cartoon characters are trying to actually do...

And sometimes you could laugh at my weirdness without going mad...

And just sometimes you could make me feel that you are always there for me...

And sometimes hold me tight for I fear dark and believe in ghosts *(Laughs)*...

And sometimes you could narrate me stories while I sleep on you...

And sometimes you could share everything with me for I can be a solution to all your problems...

And sometimes you could trust me...

And know that you mean the world to me and I could not breathe a day without you...

Just sometimes... if you could...

... but simply stare at the stars upward into the dark sky and watch with sad eyes, the twinkling of the stars stitched in the divine cloth of dark...

But is it possible for you to send down someone... so many angels... one for me???...

Lord...

Your world, your days, your nights, your rules, your ways...

Am I so gone a creation of yours?

Am I so low a being?

You hear what the wind whispers to trees and oceans to shores...

Then hear why I plead...

I am not strong to bear anymore...

Not even a little...

Get done with records of my life...

And call me back...

Or end what grieves me...

The All-Power and the All-Knowing!...

If you wish to end... then end...

Just one life is not enough to bear...

I accept what you give...

All I request is

Hurt but don't break!...

Hit but don't shatter!...

I have too little to give...

Let it be left!

But at times, I wish you could encircle me.. or hug me tight enough to make my ribs ache..

But at times, I realize how large the distance is...

And much road left to reach you...

[Sad][Sad]...

Only if God had known what you meant to me...

TBH, you miss from me...

No blood but just an empty beating heart...

Something exceptional.... when love is true nothing else matters... someone who is made for you will surely fall for you irrespective of your looks and would love you in ways you would have never dreamed about....

When he kisses me, I am a tide getting attracted to my moon...

And even if you are not here to stay...

I am happy, the universe allowed your soul stay...

With every tear that blinds mine eyes, your image is formed!.. Every moment that I break, I have the faith you would have left heavens and came near me and are revolving around me challenging the world to dare stare at me and they would know the consequences....

With every wound I take you name...

Day by day, the pain inflicted, rises, and I know that it will eat me up soon...

Not sad!... I am happy.... I smile....

I know you have gone to a world (like now people go for work to countries maybe leaving behind their loved ones promising to call them, as soon as they are settled....)...

I believe, you'll call me soon!....

A day when my heart breaks in sorrow, and when they put in mud and go back homes to sleep in bed... that day I am on my station, and you the destination!

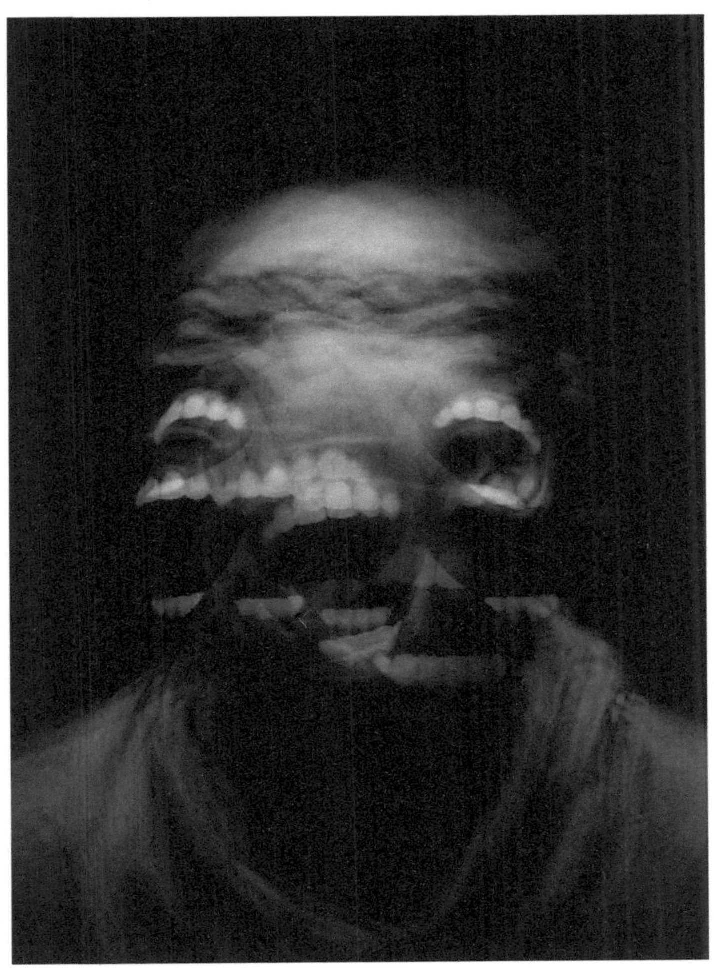

IV

Unstable

And has left me, but on whom? No forest to run, no darkness to escape, no light to blind, to steam to hide...*[Sad]*...

Did I ever desire anything much?

Did I?

but each day- I drown somewhere into non-existence!

And then when it is raining now, I am reminded more!

The fragrance that's rising from heated land...

Burns me in despair!

Let me dissolve into drops from cloud!

Carry me Oh! God to them...

Hear! [Sad]

ꝏ

Had hiccups been with the reason that someone is remembering you...

I would have been constantly involved with this exhausting activity...

It is you being Oh! My Soul...

That when you remember me.. Or when you are around...

My heart changes it's pattern of throbbing...

An indication of your call for me... *[Heart Eyes]*...

The better and most beautiful phenomenon than the occurrence of hiccups... *[Blessed]*

ꝏ

Though my eyes can no longer see you...
My heart will always feel you...

ꝏ

I never thought, I'd be helpless enough....

It was when you are, nobody dared to touch me longer than their relationship with me allowed...

When I was at peace that even my own relatives cannot hurt/scold me... When no one could shout my name... All because of you being with me...

When I was calm that whatever be you are there and you would let not anything/anyone even stare at me... That I can always run into you and you'd cover me with your hands calming me...

Now that, God has done what for him (God) was right... I stand here... tears dripping almost every day... weeping through the nights... now they shout... they know no one is there to take my stand... they are fearless to hurt... my hurt aches to an extent that maybe a day veins would burst...

Each time a thing happens... I just turn back and cry that were you there!... I did not have to hear... were you there... nobody could have said a word...

I prefer to live with you... and I do not desire anything else... I want nothing... nothing... Had you been there! Had you seen what goes through me... Had you held me... Had God acted! *[Crying]*

ꙮ

It is more than just breathing; it's intoxicating, you're like a drug to me.

I fight the desire and it keeps coming back, that I am captive, and only you can set me free.

How can this be so wrong if it feels so right? You're my vice, guilty, pleasure, my favorite sin.

I find heaven ,if there is such a place, when you are near me. I am in hell when we are apart.

You're what I need to breathe...

ꟹ

Do you know what gives me strength?

You.

Realizing that nobody can dare touch me, without your permission. Nobody. Not even my family and relatives. When I see people wanting to hand-shake and they back...

I feel blessed. I pride having you.

ꟹ

Does it matter to me if you aren't there? yea.... emptiness unfathomable... I know... along with Eid this year, you would have definitely discussed with me, what do I need on my birthday?

You know the answer, right? Have you ever seen me asking anything from you or anyone? Have you?? Then this year too...

I wish, you could hug me so tightly so as to make me loose my breath... shake hands with me holding them such, that after it's done, you could feel the numbness of my palm on yours......

From the tip of your hair to the nail of your toe... from the top of your skin till the depth of bone marrow and beyond and all... I want all of you... all... what else could be a better present?

Let me seek God and turn towards him both in despair and hope, let it not happen, that I wait for him and You permit him not!... let not it be, that, I am there looking on my birthday for him and you allow him not....

Let it be through your humbleness and might, that I could feel him enveloping me...

So what is it, that is against your power? Nothing. You are omnipotent. You are omnipresent.

Then I plead for you to hear. Hearer of all that's said in the depths of oceans where even our hands are not visible to us, hearer of all that's said on the face of oceans and on waves that strike the shore and on the air above and on the clouds that forms from the air and then on the rain that drops from the cloud to meet the rivers.... and all that's said beyond earth and galaxies and beyond distances ever heard or thought of or measured....

I bow in all submission to you... just for a day atleast... keep him and I near...

I'll never hurt you in ways I have been hurt....

And I will love you in all ways that I have never been loved...

If ever something sad has to be said... this is done...

At times there are things so painful... full of emptiness... it's unbearable...

I swear at this... i am in tears and they are flowing down my eyes to mine cheeks...

if only you could feel what did bull felt??... It lost it...

This is something which is to an extent much relatable.. At times, I feel, I cannot get out of sorrow but then now I realise at-least I can share out via posts, poetry, articles, shayaris and all...

But the bull... when he would have returned back to fight again... I am sure he would have had a final look at his owner in all helplessness...

I tell you... if someone turns towards you to seek shelter, provide them... you don't know... maybe you are everything he has... maybe you are the only hope...

They say mind is responsible for emotions... but I can assure... It pricks here in heart... it hurts here in heart...

Never play evil... Never...

If you were there, I would have never named myself... for you are were/are sufficient to love me.... and I do not need to love myself or care for myself... when I need a drop then you are oceans for me... why would I need to love myself when you are revolving around me... flowing in me...

When curtains of mine eyes would fall in peace... the day I am there in white beneath mud... after all legal proceedings done, I would burst asking angles to carry me to you and if God really cares... for I believe he does... he won't stop me... I would hug you tightly and heat of tears shall blind mine eyes... and maybe saying what you are to me I shall sleep in your arms... for it's been long I slept in peace and content....

Then show me your protection and possession like you do... and from that moment on... don't let anything reach me or touch me or hurt me or talk loudly to or shout my name....then hold my hands and tighten yours around... when then angles question... tell them, "I belong to you..." I shall cling to your chest and hear you... and then hold me, in ways like you did... do!

If truth was said.... then it is this and this is it... I want to be with you now and forever and without the delay of even a millionth part of a millisecond...

It hurts......

If you cannot do anything... do not break anything...

Everything within me is made of glass...

Every time I bend to re-collect, it pricks, makes me bleed... it hurts... *[Sad]*

V

Distracted

That i care when I have no reasons to...

That i just want to see love in your eyes....

ꕤ

Think of the moment... in which you and I are there...

Of the moment when what you say, you do...

Of the moment when you set things on fire because I am cold...

Of the moment when your anger gets instantly cooled because of my touch...

Of the moment when your lips gets me to close eyes...

ꕤ

Exactly... and you know... In a moment I can forget myself but not you... My tongue moves in prayer and the first words which are uttered are always for you... What do I ask for [from God]? You know better...

ꝏ

The thing you can love from... there is always hope... and there is always love....

ꝏ

But only if you had few drops of emotions to understand... that I wait... for I care... and I care... because I love...

and I speak not that I love... for I fear... and I fear because I feel you'll not feel me or feel what I say...

ꝏ

If I love I will love you more than anything... love you to the moon and back...

but I want your presence to be felt... if you wish... you are allowed to enter the doors of my heart... or leave... but standing at the door and making me want you is not allowed at all...

ꝏ

I would have still not stopped you... but had you said "I wish not to go."...

ꝏ

Those unmatched unparallel flow of words soaked in emotions...

ꝏ

Did I desire anything but you? Did I ever want anything near me but you? I have you and I owe the earth and heavens.

But Heavens are more dear to me. You know why? Your presence!

I miss you each day more, and every day I pass, I am a little more near you... a little more towards you... and someday you'll see... I am sitting right besides you...

God knows why am I still living... At times I feel I could end everything... everything... and run and keeping running till my soul liberates itself...

Tired of everything... every single thing...

And at times I wish I never existed! or I could run away to uncanny places where no one can ever reach out to me...

Sometimes I feel... had there been no darkness... how alone would i have been...

Lord knows LIGHT where have you been?... How I wish you were here.... Intensively remembering you these days... This moment, I could have buried myself in you...

Just need you here by me...

VI

Hysterical

And just sometimes, I wish someone could hold me by my shoulders, look into my eyes and tell me "hey, it's all okay, and I here"...

And if I could only break down in front of him...

Sad!

ꕤ

And then on this day is your birthday... All they went and yesterday's night... And none...

I just roam out with lanterns in night, torches in day, looking for you... Maybe somewhere, at some cross road I might find you...

ꕤ

Even though I am kind of strong... (Maybe)... But then, at times and only just at times, how I wish, there could have been someone to say "I am there" and really meant it...

I never thought, I'd be helpless enough....

It was when you are, nobody dared to touch me longer than their relationship with me allowed...

When I was at peace that even my own relatives cannot hurt/scold me... When no one could shout my name... All because of you being with me...

When I was calm that whatever be you are there and you would let not anything/anyone even stare at me... That I can always run into you and you'd cover me with your hands calming me...

Now that, God has done what for him (God) was right... I stand here... tears dripping almost every day... weeping through the nights... now they shout... they know no one is there to take my stand... they are fearless to hurt... My heart aches to an extent that maybe a day veins would burst...

Each time a thing happens... I just turn back and cry that were you there!... I did not have to hear... were you there... nobody could have said a word...

I prefer to live with you... and I do not desire anything else... I want nothing... nothing... Had you been there!... Had you seen what goes through me... Had you held me... Had God acted!

Does it matter to me if you aren't there? yea.... emptiness unfathomable...

I know... along with Eid this year, you would have definitely discussed with me, what do I need on my birthday?

You know the answer, right?

Have you ever seen me asking anything from you or anyone? Have you??

Then this year too...

I wish, you could hug me so tightly so as to make me loose my breath... shake hands with me holding them such, that after it's done, you could feel the numbness of my palm on yours......

From the tip of your hair to the nail of your toe... from the top of your skin till the depth of bone marrow and beyond and all... I want all of you... all... what else could be a better present?

Let me seek God and turn towards him both in despair and hope, let it not happen, that I wait for him and You permit him not!... let not it be, that, I am there looking on my birthday for him and you allow him not....

Let it be through your humbleness and might, that I could feel him enveloping me...

So what is it, that is against your power? Nothing. You are omnipotent. You are omnipresent.

Then I plead for you to hear. Hearer of all that's said in the depths of oceans where even our hands are not visible to us, hearer of all that's said on the face of oceans and on waves that strike the shore and on the air above and on the clouds that forms from the air and then on the rain that drops from the cloud to meet the rivers.... and all that's said beyond earth and galaxies and beyond distances ever heard or thought of or measured...

I bow in all submission to you... just for a day atleast... keep him and I near...

At times I realize, I actually don't have anyone with me... But had you been there, things would have been different...

When I put my hand on yours,

and look at you in wonder unable to sleep,

lost somewhere,

And I touch your cheek,

And stare in some hope of peace,

Then will you sing a lullaby?

And put me to sleep??...

You know what pricks????

It is you who made me learn to ignore...

And then it is you, who ignored...

VII
Unbalanced

I feel like Jacob, who was informed by his 11 sons (who hated Joseph) that, Joseph, fell prey to a wild animal (bear).

They handed over to him (Jacob) a cloth stained in blood as a prove to their false testament.

Jacob cried in seperation of his son Joseph so much that he went blind.

The intense the love is, the harder is to deal, and it gets more harder when you are handling everything by yourself and are constantly surrounded by people who are just adding negative to your already grief-struck state.

How far did love bring you?

When he passed away... I wasn't able to recover from that incident... I used to believe he is still alive... when I did not see him for days... I started to believe in superstitions.... I used to watch videos of how to bring a dead person back to life... read articles about it... do things anyone said or posted... tried finding people who would at least establish a contact with him... read verses or started to believe in spells...

Nothing worked. Nothing happened. So I turned towards God, whatever stories of miracles I had read... I prayed that all prophets and the appointed ones together would do some miracle for me.

Nothing worked. Nothing happened.

I haven't stopped asking him in prayers though!

There were years in my life when my life was full of love, happiness, homely satisfaction, everything one would ever want...

Those were days, when I used to pray to my God, to keep everything as it is... I used to do things so well... I used to dream of a family, of a house, of organizing dinner and living...

Now are the years, when I stand- praying again- but this time to end myself... How far did his separation take me?

I lament....
Someone call him or send me there...

How I wish I could sleep tonight and never wake up... Be dead and never see this world again...

How much do I need and miss LIGHT... I never said this before... But today, I feel, I have lost him... *[Cries]*

Why doesn't my heart stop beating?

There is absolutely nothing that I desire more than you...

And I love you so much that this is unexplainable...

A fish that says it loves the water... But you know well, for a fish, water is not just love, water is everything, this can have... It's very existence... You are water to me...

I love you in that intensity... My existence is your being... And whoever I be with on earth... In heavens, where all is pure and white... There is nothing which can keep me away from your arms and your sight... And there.... encircle me...

On that note... You are awaited...

VIII

Deranged

The jungle burns in fire whose smoke has risen to reach the skies. All I see spectators around me. There is no ambulance, no fireman. no one running with water buckets and sand, to check the plight of my organs that are choking in the smoke of absence of LIGHT.

With him there was a wall that protected... Without him, all the happy territory is invaded and looted by acute events of dark...

Had you been here, you would have seen how every sky has turned dark...

Sleepless nights, tiring days and a headache that chews my brain...

I read Jesus had a miracle to return back life and similar miracles were given to other prophets... How whole-heartedly I believe in prophets and their miracles!... Yet I am left abandoned in this desert... I am left like a bird who has travelled miles and miles without a drop of water...

Like a sharp fork tearing a piece of bread... I feel being teared and in tears...

Wouldn't LIGHT check on me? Would he not be here?... I run like a mad like someone who has been completely left in an unknown city and no directions to go...

There isn't a cage... There are thorns in them... It is not a flower... I see a dragger...

Since weeks, I am trying more than I could, putting in every effort I can to get my state back to normal...

Since last 3-4 days I have been staying good. At least I felt that probably I am getting fine. I started with doing things I used to do- slowly.

But then today, I realize, I haven't gotten better even a bit... Everything has just gone behind the epidermis of my skin... It is still there... It is still around... It is here...

Where are the humans going? If we stretch our hands, we could break them but not touch the sky. Perhaps God raised skies to make us realize how small we are. Then what is the trend of collecting black for hearts? Why is selfishness tattooed on minds?

I received a call from the very person who told me he'd be able to never call, who made me cry, broke me, and everything. Months after he taught I wouldn't be of need, now he needs help with his presentation- and so he talked sweet. I know his mind now, so I just guided. My heart has lost connections with him.

I saw at some place, some people trying to balance themselves over some sphere or a rolling object. They eventually fall. I read in geography- earth is similar- oblate spheroid. I checked in philosophy- life is rolling. We all will eventually fall in mud.

Then wouldn't it be alright, if we all had love in our hearts and cared for each other, instead of just looking at own interests?

IX

Insane

Like an animal whose throat has been cut off with a blunt knife...

I look around at the world with broken eyes...

In pain I wail today...

LIGHT, come back, hold me and stay...

Day by day, it is getting unbearable... Where have all my people gone? Why I am not able to see [anyone]?

This pain in my heart is eating me up like termites eat wood....

LIGHT save me.... Send your help oh God...

All my peace has vanished, Oh LIGHT, if only you could see that the eyes that slept in peace, now stay awake- borthered through the night...

Had you been- such are the torments that I could have sit with you- hugging you... Why doesn't this journey comes to an end?

ꕤ

How hard it keeps getting when your heart is bursting? No matter the care some of you sent, can someone send me LIGHT? .... I am extremely hurt (at levels I cannot describe)...

ꕤ

I see some people who congratulate me. I do not find, anyone who is willing to sit by my side, who can pierce through my eyes, peep into my heart. See- there is nothing fine in it. I wish LIGHT lived with me or took me along with him to heavens....

ꕤ

I have always found my life circling. From where I start, I return back to the same point, in spite of wanting to move ahead.

ꕤ

In times of despair I lost my drug-box...
It became so dark that everything was visible...

ꕤ

You presence was a veil of silk for my life...
In your absence I see all burned holes in it...
You were there, mine eyes used to shine...

In light now I see only darkness...
You were here, it was as if there was a flower in a dried up field...
Now I see only pebbles and stones...
Like someone lost in a fair, I search for you...
I see only animals around...
Your seperation is a war of what kind?
Whenever I begin fighting, I always loose...

ℵ

Light, Your seperation is a war of what kind for me? Whenever I want to fight, I loose... Your seperation? See, where it has led me... If you were here, I would have narrated to you... The eyes which shone in your presence, have now gone blind...
Is there a road? that I could run to reach you... With what intensity, I look for you in corners of my life, buring my heart as a candle?

ℵ

I used to believe that it was angles who put flowers on plants... One day, when I was really hurt... I took a paper, with pen, I wrote complains to my father on it and expressed how I got physically hurt and how I am existing...

I buried that chit in soil secretly, hoping when angles come, they are going to take it away and give it to father... So he would return back, save me, and scold them...

I waited for a reply... It did not came, I dug up the soil after few days, my paper wasn't there... I was convinced it reached him...

When he did not come even after weeks, I thought I am a bad child and probably I was at mistake, so I said sorry in prayers even without knowing any reasons for it... And dealt with things on my own...

When I got older, read about environment... I realized that paper of complains never reached him... It just got degraded in soil...

That's how important I found LIGHT... He gave me strength... Gone are those days, when I used to see him around... How much I wish, I could run into him today... I am almost back into same state... LIGHTTT... How do I call you from heavens?

These lugubrious posts of mine, go unseen by the creator and creation alike. Where do I find my way? Where is the street that takes me up?

X

Neurotic

I have read in scriptures, Jesus was given this miracle that he could bring back people to life. Lord of Jesus, am I so woebegone, still my prayers do not seem to be answered?

ꙮ

In verses they say heart aches when in pain...

I am actually feeling those sharp stings of pain... Like real pain...

I am constantly loosing all control over me with every passing hour...

ꙮ

What does a bee do when it doesn't find a flower. All the flower fields in front of my eyes are dried up. Solitary, I go from one point to another. Who plucked away the only flower I had?

Hear me Oh Lord. Help.

ꕥ

Take a kid to a place he has never been before. You go away for a while without letting him know. Just watch from a distance how he is trying to find you. How confused he is! How he looks towards his right and left. How he takes few step and then returns back to the very spot you left him on.

This is how I am looking for him.

ꕥ

I was a good painting on a canvas. Time took a bucket full of water filtered from nerves in my eyes, and threw it on the canvas. All colors flowed away. I turned into a scribble.

ꕥ

How hard is living without breathing? He is my breath. I grasp for air, my heart beats drum... Where is he in skies/ heavens? Where do I find him? LIGHT, return, and stand in-front of me. You used to watch me for minutes. See me now, I am dead without you.

ꕥ

Am I broken? No. I am teared.

ꕥ

When temperature outside is making people sweat. I am not feeling that, I am feeling weightlessness and no strength.

ꕥ

Take a balloon. Fill it with air. Take a pin. Just touch the balloon with it. Do you see how the balloon crumbles?

That's my state.

I so wish LIGHT was here, I could have hid myself in him. Prayers made are answered by Lord, I have been praying each day for around eight years straight. Is my application lost?

I have heard some people say, life is a battlefield. I am send to fight without armors or anything. I am standing and being hit even by the winds.

XI

Demented

A bird whose wings and body are hit hard, who has been caught, who has been hungry, who has been looked at from outside it's cage, who has been afraid of humans around it...

That bird is me. They hear me sing? Nobody hears, that I am out of misery chirping in low voices. I run like mad. I get hit against the walls made of iron bars. Every bar that touches me, I chirp with helplessness- LIGHT LIGHT...

The world hears melody. I chirp my misery.

If only he was there with me!

I have desperately wanted him to be there. His number flashes my mind, I cannot call him.

How unfortunate it is, that earth has network reach till 5G, yet there isn't a way to make a call in heavens!

He used to look at me with all love and concern and calmed me down, saying he is there always with me.... and he would never let anything reach me but smiles...

Where is him? He who said he won't even let my eyes go wet- for anything; now when my eyes are loaded with hot water filtered out of my blood... I don't see him around... Is it because of the blindness my tears brought with them?

The more deep you go in oceans, the darker it gets... I have been drowning and do not know how to swim my way out.... The last part visible- is a hand... With hopes, I go deeper... My soul is burning for torch... I cannot see anything... Does he sees me?

God, is it not in your power to return just one person for me? Where did he go?

In big big planet... With strange faces... I am running with a photo in my memory... Everyone I come across- with a broken heart, I ask, "has anyone seen him?"...

I have been carrying some blank pages, drawing maps on my own... I have been walking so much, that I am lost...

I feel as if a net of harsh wires was placed around me... The world caught me like they catch a parrot, secluding him from skies and my people....

And then that parrot being carried from time to time to be placed in a cage so small that it is hard even to turn your face...

I, like a parrot in this largely small cage, blench out of inability... Looking with eyes full of desire at the skies.... Chirping- LIGHT LIGHT... ... (If only he could be here)...

ꟸ

Where is the world?

ꟸ

I have woke up at this hour when i usually don't... I cannot sleep through nights any more...

ꟸ

Each point in body has had its stay... Angles of after-life... When shall you be here?....

Broken like cannot be repaired...

ꟸ

Those eyes that sparkled when you were around are now blind because of tears...

Lord, send him back... Send him back...

ꟸ

XII
Troubled

LIGHT look down on earth.... See where I have taken myself...

ஐ

I am sitting on terrace, staring blankly at the sky... In some hope that God is going to stretch his hand out to me...

I have believed in Him, He protects... Angles, let Him know of my state.... Come down, to gather me... I have been dismantled...

ஐ

When you look on the planet... And see far far away, the world is so crowded?... When you look on your sides , the world is but an empty vessel.... If only you could return from heaven and see me, LIGHT....

ஐ

When your rib cage is nothing more but a cage... How does this heart escape? Trapped in ribs is heart... Trapped in flesh are ribs..

ꕤ

How does it feel when you loose control over your own self?

ꕤ

As if some nerves in my heart are made up of the lightest thread possible... A simple blow and everything within crumbles while the soul stretches out to reach the skies...

ꕤ

Like a little child, lost in a fair, I run in random directions shouting LIGHT LIGHT and Lord Lord, then I hide myself behind some swing to protect myself. When I see night approaching, I look up at the skies, waiting anxiously, waiting for them to come and take me along with them. Every little nerve of my heart breaks with each passing second.

Before dawn, I rise up, look around, cannot see- neither him nor God- All frightened, startled, I again stand up and start running in random directions- shouting LIGHT LIGHT and god god, till I get tired, and then again hide myself behind a swing. I have been lost in this fair of life for years now. How do I return back home? When I ever return? When?

ꕤ

There are people who write how ending life is no solution. I wonder in the back of my head, do these people also realize how hard living is when you are constantly loosing on yourself and getting dragged in darkness where there are ghosts of past- that are haunting you and eating your flesh.

Do these people who are "strong" to deal with their tasks, ever realize how a cloth gets wet when tears are constantly flowing. Such that, the cloth doesn't anymore wipes your eyes but instead wet your cheeks when you use it.

There is a whirlpool of emotions in my heart... A chaos in my mind... A need in my soul... A longing for something... Between all this there is an intuition, at something is going to be right soon...

I always thought people give way to reason, remain on a point, but they don't.

I assumed, that everyone is a human, feels and has love. Nobody. Nobody has.

I guess there are certain people who could stab without a thought.

When I compare them with people I personally know, there is such a huge difference. So much.

Completely shocked!

My being here has given so much different aspects of people. I would have hardly ever found.

I guess devil has taken human forms and defames humanity.

Printed by Libri Plureos GmbH in Hamburg, Germany